THE Elves AND THE Shoemaker

Retold by ERIC SUBEN
Illustrated by LLOYD BLOOM

A GOLDEN BOOK • NEW YORK
Western Publishing Company, Inc., Racine, Wisconsin 53404

Once upon a time there was a kind shoemaker. Though he worked very hard, he grew so poor that at last he had only enough leather left for one pair of shoes.

One winter night he cut out the shoes, but he was too tired to finish them. He left the leather on his workbench and decided to make the shoes the next morning.

The shoemaker didn't know what he and his wife would do now that all the leather was used up, for he had no money to buy more. But despite their troubles, the shoemaker and his wife slept soundly that night.

Early the next morning, the shoemaker woke up and got dressed. He went into the shop to make his last pair of shoes.

He picked up his hammer and sat down at his workbench.

The shoemaker thought he must be dreaming. He blinked his eyes. He blinked them again. But it was no dream—on the very spot where he had left the leather the night before, there was a finished pair of beautiful, perfectly made shoes.

He called his wife into the shop and showed her the shoes. "They're splendid!" she exclaimed. "But when did you make them?"

"I didn't make them," the shoemaker replied. "I just found them here."

The shoemaker put the shoes in the window, hoping that someone would buy them. Soon the door swung open and a fine gentleman walked into the shop.

"I must have those wonderful shoes," he said. "I've never seen any like them. The stitches are so small and delicate!"

The shoemaker sold the shoes to the gentleman, who paid a very high price for them.

With the money the shoemaker was able to buy
enough leather for two more pairs of shoes. He had
enough left over to buy a soup bone for dinner.

That night he cut out the leather. But he was very
hungry, and he could smell the soup his wife was
cooking. "I'll make the shoes tomorrow," he said, and
he went to eat dinner.

The next morning he found two pairs of elegant shoes on his workbench. He showed them to his wife. "Who can be making these marvelous shoes?" she said.

The shoemaker wondered, too. Once again he placed the shoes in the window and again he didn't have long to wait before the door swung open. This time there were two customers, and they both paid the shoemaker handsomely for the shoes.

Now the shoemaker had enough money to buy leather for four pairs of shoes.

Things went on this way for some time. Every night the shoemaker cut the leather and went to sleep. And every morning he found more beautiful shoes on his workbench.

The shoemaker was growing rich.

One evening the shoemaker said to his wife, "It's nearly Christmas, and we still don't know who is making the shoes. We cannot go another day without finding out who is helping us."

So together the shoemaker and his wife thought of a plan. Instead of going to sleep that night, they hid behind a curtain in the shop.

At midnight, two tiny elves came into the room.
The shoemaker and his wife watched in amazement
as the elves stitched and sewed and hammered.

Soon the bench was filled with shiny new shoes.
The moment their work was finished, the elves
vanished.

"It's astonishing!" gasped the shoemaker's wife.

"It's miraculous!" the shoemaker agreed. "We must do something for those tiny creatures who have been so kind to us."

"Well," said his wife, "the poor little things had no coats or hats or shoes on, and they must get very cold at this time of year."

So the shoemaker and his wife made two tiny
suits of clothing for the elves.

The next night they laid the things they had made
on the table and once again hid behind the curtain.

Just at midnight, the elves came into the room.
When they saw the clothes, they were overjoyed.
They tried them on and found that they fit just right.

The elves danced all around the room and sang a merry song.

At last the elves danced out the door, never to return.

But the shoemaker and his wife, who had paid back kindness with kindness, never wanted for anything, and they lived happily for a good long time.